This book belongs to

_____

# Disney

# Winnie the Pooh

*My Book*
*of*
*Winnie the Pooh*

# PaRRagon

Bath • New York • Singapore • Hong Kong • Cologne • Delhi
Melbourne • Amsterdam • Johannesburg • Auckland • Shenzhen

*Pooh's Friends*, written by Kathleen Weidner Zoehfeld, illustrated by Studio Orlando.
Copyright © 2010 Disney Enterprises, Inc.

*Find a Friend*, illustrated by Orlando de la Paz and Paul Lopez.
Copyright © 2010 Disney Enterprises, Inc.

*Numbers*, written by Lisa Ann Marsoli, illustrated by Lori Tyminski and Atelier Phillippe Harchy.
Copyright © 2010 Disney Enterprises, Inc.

*Colors*, produced by Rocket Books, Inc.
Copyright © 2010 Disney Enterprises, Inc.

*Shapes*, written by Andrea Doering, illustrated by Angel Rodriguez.
Copyright © 2010 Disney Enterprises, Inc.

*Pooh's Day*, written by Ellen Milnes, illustrated by Angel and Eva Rodriguez.
Copyright © 2010 Disney Enterprises, Inc.

*Pooh's Honey Tree* written by Isabel Gaines, illustrated by Nancy Stevenson.
Copyright © 2010 Disney Enterprises, Inc.

This edition published by Parragon in 2011
Parragon
Queen Street House
4 Queen Street
Bath BA1 1HE, UK
www.parragon.com

Copyright © 2011 Disney Enterprises, Inc.

Based on the 'Winnie the Pooh' works, by A.A. Milne and E.H. Shepard

ISBN 978-1-4454-2681-5

Printed in China

# Contents

# Pooh's Honey Tree

Winnie the Pooh had a big, round tummy.
Pooh's tummy was always quite hungry.

Hungry for honey!

"Oh bother!" said Pooh, looking in his honeypot.
Empty.

Just then, Pooh heard a sound.

BUZZ! BUZZ! BUZZ!

Something small and fuzzy flew past his ear.
BUZZ! BUZZ! BUZZ!

"Oh!" said Pooh. "A bee!"

Pooh followed the bee.
Soon they came to
a honey tree!

Up the tree Pooh went. Up. Up. Up.

Then, *CRACK!* A branch broke.
Down the tree Pooh fell.
Down.
Down.
Down.

Pooh rubbed his sore head.

Pooh needed help.

He went to
Christopher Robin's
house. He saw that
his friend had a
big blue balloon.

"May I borrow your balloon?" Pooh asked.

"Here, Pooh," said Christopher Robin, giving him the balloon.

"Thank you," said Pooh. "I'm going to use this balloon to float up to a honey tree."

"Silly old bear," said Christopher Robin.
"The bees will not let you near their honey."
At that, Pooh sat down in the mud and rolled
around.

"Look!" said Pooh. "The bees will think I'm a little black rain cloud. They will not even know I am there."

Christopher Robin sat down to see
what would happen next.

Pooh held on to the balloon. He floated up
to the top of the honey tree.

Pooh reached into the bees' nest and pulled out a pawful of golden honey.

BUZZ! BUZZ! BUZZ! The bees did not think that Pooh was a little black rain cloud. They thought he was a hungry bear!

Suddenly, the balloon string came undone and the air swooshed out!

Pooh and his balloon sailed over the treetops.

Finally the balloon lost
all its air. Down it came.
And down came Pooh.

Pooh landed right in Christopher Robin's arms!
Pooh looked up at the bees in the tree. Then he
looked at Christopher Robin. "Oh dear!" Pooh said.
"I guess it all comes from liking honey so much!"

# Pooh's Friends

The most wonderful
thing about
**Piglets**

is Piglets are
huggable things.

The most wonderful
thing about
**Tiggers**

is Tiggers are made out of springs.

The most wonderful
thing about
Eeyores
is the way they
make life sunny.

The most wonderful
thing about
Rabbits
is their pantries are
filled up with honey.

The most wonderful
thing about
**Kangas**
is the time they
share with Roo.

The most wonderful
thing about
**Roos**
is the generous
things that they do.

The most wonderful
thing about
**Owls**
is the stories they
tell every day.

The most wonderful
thing about
**friends**
is the love they
bring our way!

# Find a friend

Pooh and all of his friends
pictured below appear in
the scene on the next page.
Can you point to them all?

Roo

Kanga

Tigger

Pooh

Piglet

Owl

Rabbit

Eeyore

# Numbers

**1** **One**
happy
butterfly
dancing in
the sky.

**2** **Two** great big acorns
to make an acorn pie.

# 3
## Three

pots of honey
will make
a special
treat.

# 4
## Four

bags of carrots
for all the
friends
to eat.

# 5 Five giant bouncing balls, lined up in a row.

# 6
## Six
pretty yellow kites with orange tails in tow.

# 7
## Seven
purple flowers
in a little
spotted pot.

# 8
## Eight
books of
stories – now
that's a lot.

# 9
## Nine
red and blue balloons.
Hip, hip, hooray!

# 10 Ten friends to celebrate a Hundred-Acre day.

# Colours

Five little honeypots all in a line,

Pooh reached
for the
**yellow**
one and said,
"It's dinnertime!"

Four little honeypots all full of honey,

Pooh picked up the
## red
pot next.
Look at Pooh's big
tummy!

Three little honeypots all in a row,

Pooh reached for the **purple** pot.
Two more pots to go.

Two little honeypots, one green, the other blue,

Pooh took down the **green** pot
and emptied that one, too.

One little honeypot alone up on the shelf,

"Oh dear!" said hungry Pooh.
"The **blue** pot's by itself!"

Five little honeypots, sitting on the floor.
"Mmmm!" Pooh said happily.
"I wish I had some more!"

# Shapes

There's a party today for Winnie the Pooh!
Let's tag along and learn shapes, too.

Tigger's bouncy, bouncing ball
flies through the air – now watch it fall!

# square

Eeyore's gift is bright and blue.
These blocks will be a treat for Pooh.

rectangle

Rabbit is a practical friend –
"A tea towel is the gift to send."

diamond

Owl wisely brings a kite.
"Now, don't forget to hold on tight!"

The bright new sail sways and swings
on the present Christopher Robin brings.

The heart-shaped card addressed to Pooh
is signed with love from little Roo.

heart

oval

Piglet has the perfect present –
"This pink balloon is very pleasant."

star

Just as his birthday is almost gone,
Pooh spots a star for wishing on.
But he tells his pals, "With friends like you,
All my wishes have come true."

# Pooh's Day

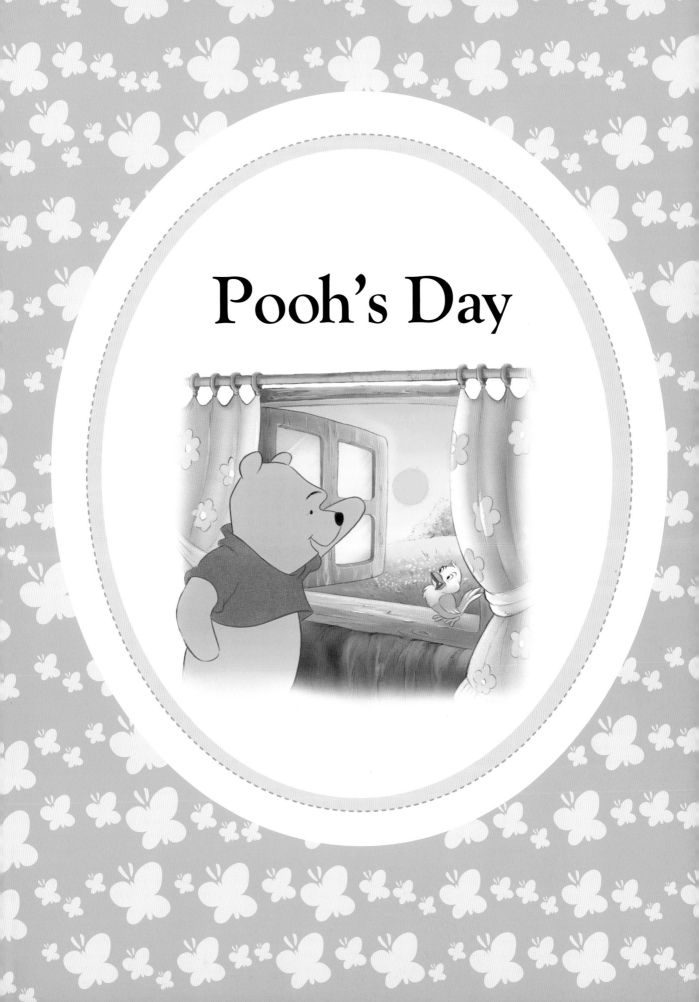

# Wake-Up Time

As soon as the sunshine
says hello,
Pooh Bear makes his bed.
He wiggles his nose
and touches his toes,
and sings little songs in
his head.

# Playtime

In the middle of the morning
Pooh goes out to play.
He has a swing,
pretends he's king,
and looks forward to his day.

# Lunchtime

Every single day at noon
Pooh Bear eats his honey.
Sometimes he slurps,
and then he burps.
He always thinks that's funny!

# Craft Time

Some days after eating lunch,
Pooh has a craft to start.
He paints a flower
for a happy hour.
It's fun to make art.

# Nap Time

Every sleepy afternoon
Pooh Bear takes a nap.
He dreams of things
with whistles and wings
that go "rap-a-tap-tap, a-tap-tap."

# Dinnertime

While the sun is still awake,
Pooh sits down to eat.
He says a blessing
about honey dressing
and a world so sunny and sweet.

# Story Time

Just before the sun disappears
Pooh turns on the light.
He looks at books
about princes and crooks
and things that go bump
in the night.

# Bath Time

Every night when it gets dark
Pooh climbs into the tub.
He cleans his ears
so he can hear
and sings,
"Rub-dub-rub-dub-rub-dub."

# Bedtime

When the sky is full of stars
Pooh Bear goes to sleep.
He closes his eyes
and wonders why
his head is full of sheep!

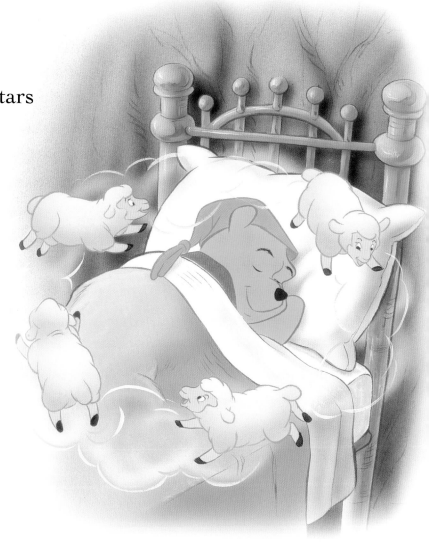